Walt Disney Presents

EL BLANCO—THE LEGEND OF THE
White Stallion

by RUTHERFORD MONTGOMERY

Illustrated by Gloria Stevens

SCHOLASTIC BOOK SERVICES

NEW YORK · TORONTO · LONDON · AUCKLAND · SYDNEY · TOKYO

ISBN 0-590-03129-5

Copyright © 1961 by Walt Disney Productions. This edition is published by Scholastic Book Services, a division of Scholastic Inc., 730 Broadway, New York, NY 10003, by arrangement with Walt Disney Productions.

24 23 22 21 20 19 18 17 16   2 3 4 5 6/8
                        Printed in the U. S. A.   11

Contents

For

Hillary Hecathorn

Introduction

The Legend
and the Miracle

For CENTURIES, the mountains of Mexico have
looked down on man. Under their high peaks
great kingdoms have grown and decayed and died,
leaving behind only ruins of cities and temples.

On a slope overlooking a deep valley in central
Mexico, there still stand the roofless walls of one
such temple — a temple built as a shrine to El
Blanco, the white stallion.

The ancient people of Mexico were Indians. Long before the temple was built, they told stories of a white god who would appear some day, mounted on a strange beast. And when the Spaniard Hernando Cortez came to their country, they believed he was the white god. They had never seen a horse, and they believed that Cortez's white stallion was also a kind of god. Cortez encouraged these beliefs. El Blanco had become lame, and Cortez left the horse with the village priests. He would return for it later, after the lameness was cured.

That same day a furious storm came up, ending a long drought. The priests thought that El Blanco had brought the rains, and they called him the master of storm and lightning. Knowing nothing about horses, they fed him the spiced food they ate themselves and gave him wine to drink. El Blanco soon sickened and died. The priests then built the temple, and within it, on a block of stone, they placed a statue of the white stallion. They prayed to it and made offerings to it. They were sure that if a long drought came again, El Blanco would return, bringing the rain.

On the walls of the temple they painted three pictures. The first showed Cortez delivering the lame stallion to them. The second showed El Blanco summoning the storm. The third showed the life-sized statue. In time the people gave up their gods and became Christians. The statue was smashed. But the three pictures, scarred and mossy, remain to this day — and so does the legend of the white stallion that brings the rain.

Now there was a great need for El Blanco to return. Little rain had fallen for several seasons. The corn had withered, and most of the wells and springs were dry. The people who lived in the village near the ruins of the temple moved away. Only the old man, a descendant of one of the temple priests, stayed on. He lived in a one-room adobe shack, and his companion was Croppy, his aged burro.

The Trap

ONE HOT AFTERNOON, as usual, the old man carried water from a spring at the temple to his small patch of corn. He believed that this spring still gave water because it was at the shrine of the white stallion. After chopping the weeds from around the cornstalks, he had no more work to do. The sun beat down on him as he leaned on his hoe, gazing dreamily into the valley. It was really a box canyon, with one narrow entrance through the cliffs above his house and another at the lower end of the valley. It was an ideal place for wild horses, and indeed a band of them lived there. The wild horses were the old man's hope. Surely one of the mares would give birth to a white stallion, and then the rains would come. Although the old man was a Christian, the ancient legend meant much to him. And his faith in the tale of El Blanco kept him there on the parched, dying land.

The old man saw the band of horses break out of a grove of trees in the valley, and his eyes lit up. The mares and colts ran swiftly, followed by the herd stallion. He drove the herd across the valley in a way that worried the old man. It was plain that the stallion sensed danger and was lashing at the mares to make them stampede to safety. Something was chasing the horses, but the dust raised by their hoofs kept the old man from seeing what it was. He watched them gallop up the steep slope toward the temple. They charged past it and swerved, heading down toward the opening in the rocky wall of the canyon.

It was then that the old man saw three men on horseback galloping after the herd. Wild-horse hunters! They must have built a trap in the canyon below, knowing that the herd stallion would try to escape that way. Suddenly the old man felt tired, and he gripped his hoe handle tightly. Turning slowly, he walked to his house and sank down on the doorstone. His hope was gone. There would be no white colt to grow into a stallion and bring the rain.

He sat for a long time in front of his little house, watching the band of wild horses vanish into the canyon below. He did not have to see the cunning trap built in the narrow passage. He knew it was there, and that the stallion and all of the mares would be caught. When the three hunters, too, had disappeared in the canyon, his eyes turned toward the ruins of the temple.

The old man was a good Christian who made regular pilgrimages to the little church in the village far below the valley. But the beliefs of his ancestors were also part of his life. It seemed natural to him that the spirits which had watched over the white stallion should still live in the temple. Perhaps he should go there, and let them know that he had no part in what was taking place in the valley now.

Getting to his feet, the old man went slowly across the slope. He walked erect, with his head held high. In all the seventy years of his life he had walked with his head held high. Now his steps were slower and his body was no longer powerful. But his eyes were clear, and he needed no staff to steady himself.

Near the temple, the old man stopped. For a moment he lowered his head in reverence, as he always did before climbing over the low barrier which blocked the temple's entrance. He closed his eyes and crossed his hands over his heart. Suddenly he opened his eyes. Rain, coming down in big drops, was pelting his back and neck. A gust of wind whipped off his sombrero and sent it spinning toward the temple wall. The old man just stood and let the rain drench him. He did not even pull his serape close around him to keep his body dry. The coming of this life-giving rain, so badly needed, was beyond understanding.

Moving slowly, he walked toward the temple wall to pick up his sombrero. Water dripped from his mass of white hair and streamed down his face. He licked his lips eagerly and sucked in the tiny rivulets of water. Bending over, he picked up the sombrero. It was a long time since the old hat had been soaked with rain water. As he straightened up again, he faced a jagged opening in the temple wall where a number of stones had fallen out. He looked in through the opening and gasped.

Inside the temple, sheltered by one wall, stood a mare. And on the floor near her lay a newly born white colt. The mare lowered her muzzle and gently nudged the colt. Using all his strength, the colt pulled his feet together, stood up, and, stretching out his neck, drank deeply of his mother's milk.

The old man watched breathlessly, filled with a great joy. Here at last was the miracle he had been waiting for! Here was the white stallion, and with it had come the rain.

The old man hurried to the entrance, climbed over the barrier, and stood looking at the colt. The wild mare was frightened, but she would not bolt

and leave her foal. The old man talked to her softly in Spanish, moving closer as he talked. The mare trembled, but did not move. There was something in the old man's voice that calmed her.

"You have need for food," the old man said. "I will bring corn from my field." He put his hand on the colt. "You are El Blanco, the spirit of the storm."

El Blanco pulled his head from under his mother's flank and looked at the old man. He had no fear of humans. He had been born just three hours ago and had not yet learned to fear anything. But he was curious, and he stretched out his damp muzzle. The old man stroked it. The mare nickered a warning, and El Blanco drew his muzzle back. He pressed against his mother's side, and the old man smiled.

Leaving the temple, the old man went to his cornfield. The rain had stopped, and the earth was wet. The cornstalks were stunted, sad-looking things, but already the curled leaves had started to unroll. The old man cut an armload of stalks with his machete. Although he needed every ear the field could produce for his own use, he did not hesitate. El Blanco came first.

On his way back to the temple, the old man thought about the problem of saving the mare and colt from the hunters. It would not be easy. He was sure that the mare had been with the wild herd when the hunters started their drive. She must have dropped out of the herd as it passed the temple, seeking a spot where her foal could be born in safety.

The old man was also sure that the hunters had counted the herd. It was not a large one. The hunters would know that one mare was missing, and would come looking for her. If she stayed in the temple, she might yet escape. There was a spring there from which she could drink, but her only food would be the old man's corn, which he could not spare. On the other hand, if she went into the valley to graze, the hunters would see her.

The old man was still thinking about the problem as he put the corn before the mare. He could lead her out through the upper entrance of the valley and send her down into the wilderness, which stretched as far west as the jungle. But he could not do it immediately, for the little stallion was not strong enough for such a journey. While the mare sniffed hungrily at the green corn, the

old man made up his mind. Just as soon as the
colt could travel, he would take them both out of
the valley.

The old man slept soundly that night. When
he was a young man, he had formed the habit of
not worrying about his troubles. Worry never
solved anything, and a man had to face each day
as it came.

Next morning, he was up very early to carry
more cornstalks to the temple. He was pleased to
see that the mare had eaten all the corn he had left

the evening before. And he was pleased, too, by El Blanco's friskiness. The colt was bouncing about in a lively manner. If the two horses could be kept out of sight for this one day, the young colt would surely be strong enough for the trip out of the valley.

The old man was sunning himself on his doorstone when Lopez, the leader of the wild-horse hunters, came riding into the yard. He was a stocky man with broad shoulders and a pleasant enough face. Hunting had been poor for a long time, and he wanted to capture every one of the wild horses. After taming them, he would sell them for a good price in the ranch country to the north. He knew of no reason to let any get away; the horses were wild and belonged to whoever could catch them. He would have laughed at the idea that a white stallion could bring rain. He had grown up in a town, away from the people who remembered the ancient stories.

The old man watched Lopez ride up from the valley, and he intended to keep watching him. He hoped that the hunter would give up the search if he saw no sign of the mare. Lopez reined his horse to a stop and smiled down at the old man.

"A beautiful morning, old man," he said.

"It is indeed," the old man answered softly, more to himself than to the stranger Lopez.

"You have been sitting here all morning?"

"Since very early," the old man said.

"You have perhaps seen a mare in the valley?"

The old man looked calmly at Lopez. "I have seen no mare in the valley," he said.

"This mare was heavy with foal. She must have slipped away from the herd to find a place to bear her colt." Lopez spread his hands wide. "With so much dust smothering me and my riders, she went unseen."

"She is perhaps in the woods below," the old man said.

"My men searched the woods after the rain yesterday." Lopez turned and looked with interest at the temple. "She might have entered those ruins."

"There is no roof for shelter, and only rocks and rubble to eat," the old man answered.

"Yes, she would be hungry there," Lopez said. "But I can look to make sure."

The old man said thoughtfully, "Without grass to eat, the mare would long since have left the ruin. She would also seek water."

"That is very true," Lopez agreed.

"You are sure one mare is missing? You say there was much dust, and wild horses run fast, dodging back and forth. I hunted them in my youth, and often I counted poorly." The old man leaned back and sighed, as though thinking of his youth.

"You are perhaps right. I waste time looking for a mare that does not exist." Lopez lifted a hand. "*Adios,* old one. I have much hard work to do, taming the horses I have caught." He whirled his horse around and galloped down the slope.

The old man smiled as he watched Lopez ride away. He said softly to himself, "He is gone, and I do not have a lie on my soul. I spoke only the truth."

Escape

THE NEXT MORNING the old man spent a full half-hour watching the valley below for riders. He saw nothing of Lopez or his men, and was satisfied that they had given up the search for the mare. But he knew that Lopez would come back, because this sheltered and protected valley was an ideal haven for wild horses. There was always a chance some stallion would discover the valley and bring in a herd. The old man decided to get the white stallion away at once, before Lopez returned for a last look.

The old man slipped a rope bridle on Croppy, and led the burro up to the temple. Over his arm he carried a halter. The mare was still inside the stone walls, but she was showing signs of restlessness. El Blanco was very lively, and welcomed the old man by kicking up his heels. The old man talked softly to the mare. She shook her head and shied away. It was not until he had worked patiently for an hour that he was able to slip the halter over her head. She was a very fine and beautiful animal. The old man suspected that she had been stolen by the herd stallion from one of the large haciendas to the north. She carried no brand, but she might have been stolen before her owners got around to branding her.

The old man helped El Blanco over the barrier, and at once the colt became interested in Croppy. He dashed up to the old burro in spite of his mother's warning, and thrust out his muzzle. Except for cocking one ear forward, Croppy ignored the colt. The old man stood close to the temple wall while he scanned the valley below. He would have to risk moving across the open slope for at least half a mile. Once he reached the defile leading up to the rim, he and the two horses would be safely hidden from anyone riding in the valley.

He started off, keeping the mare moving as fast as his old legs would carry him. Even if he had been young and spry he could not have traveled any faster, because Croppy never moved fast. They were halfway across the open slope when the old man saw a rider lope out of the canyon below. He tried to hurry, but Croppy refused to increase his pace. Finally the old man mounted the burro and thumped his shaggy flanks. Croppy groaned, but he increased his pace to a trot. The old man had at least a quarter of a mile to go. He looked back and saw the rider heading up into the timber on the far side of the valley.

Just before they reached the rim of the defile, the old man saw the rider halt. At this distance the old man could not tell whether or not the rider was looking up toward the spot where he was leading the mare. He knew that movement always attracts attention, but he had to risk it. He sent

Croppy over the rim and down into the defile. If the rider spotted them, he would soon come galloping after them.

The defile was a narrow corridor which sloped steeply upward. On one side there was a steep bank; on the other side rose towering cliffs. Croppy climbed slowly up the rock-strewn passageway. He and the mare were sure-footed, but El Blanco was not used to such rough going. He had trouble getting over the loose boulders. His mother urged him along by nickering, almost as though she knew they must make haste.

The rim and the pass were just above them, but Croppy's lungs and scrawny legs were weakening. The old man had to halt and let the burro blow and recover a bit. It was then that he heard the ring of hoofbeats striking the rocky ground. An unseen rider was coming toward him fast.

The old man thumped Croppy's flanks, and they moved upward. They seemed to be creeping along. They would never make it to the top before the rider saw them. The old man dismounted and quickly slipped the halter off the mare. Stepping back, he lashed her hard across her sleek rump with the halter. The mare leaped away and ran up the steep slope, with El Blanco bounding after her.

The mare kept running, setting a pace which the colt could follow. The old man sat sadly watching them disappear through the pass. Looking back, he saw the rider appear on the rim below. He could probably see the defile from there. Onward went the old man, and up, toward the pass. He did not turn back, for he felt the rider watching him.

Finally he reached the pass, and rode out on the high rim which overlooked the wilderness. He sat studying the meadows and groves below, but saw nothing of the mare and the white stallion. After a while, though, the rider appeared. He pulled up beside the old man and gave him a suspicious look. The old man was glad it was not Lopez. This man looked dull, like a person with little imagination.

"What are you doing up here, old fellow?" he asked.

"I often come here." The old man swept a hand toward the high peaks to the west. "The view has much beauty, senor."

"I thought you were trailing a horse."

"Do you see a horse?" the old man asked. He was glad that he had tossed the halter behind a rock when he released the mare.

The rider scowled. The old man certainly didn't have a horse with him; nor was there a horse anywhere in sight. The rider studied the country

below for a long time, while the old man waited patiently, pretending to admire the beauty of the rugged peaks. As he waited, the old man silently made a prayer; he asked the guardian spirits who watched over the white stallion to keep the little one well hidden in the trees below. At last the rider turned and left, without another word.

The old man sat for a long time, watching the

land below. Once he thought he saw a white speck near a stand of big trees; he hoped it was El Blanco. If it *was*, then the mare was heading down into the wilderness. He watched a while longer, and then pulled Croppy around and headed back through the pass.

As he re-entered the defile, he saw the rider on a rim below. The man had waited, thinking the old man might have concealed the mare he sought.

There was no mare, so he rode away.

The old man rode sadly on down the defile. He hoped that some day the white stallion would return — perhaps when he was fully grown. With the god of storm in the valley, the land would never have another drought.

Wilderness

EL BLANCO'S MOTHER sensed danger in roaming the wild country alone with her foal. He could not run fast, and he needed to be watched constantly. Otherwise he would stray into thickets or dense groves of trees where a killer might be lurking. The mare had been a herd mare for so long that she had come to depend on the leadership of a stallion who was always alert for danger, and ready to attack any wolf or big cat that tried to stalk the herd. So she kept moving deeper into the wilderness, searching for a herd of mares that she could join.

El Blanco was carefree and happy. He was well fed, and continually seeing and meeting new things. Full of high spirits, he liked to frolic in the meadow grass and run with the wind.

That first night the mare picked a resting spot in the open, yet close to a grove of trees. She had considered the grove itself, then decided against it. There was too much tangled underbrush beneath the trees. Out in the open she could see any animal that tried to creep up on her foal. El Blanco lay down, and she stood over him. The stars shone brightly overhead.

Night sounds were different from those El Blanco had heard during the day. Even the air smelled different. The wind that had been blowing across the fragrant pines had died down, and now in place of the wind's song came the trilling of a million insects.

Some of the night sounds frightened El Blanco and gave him his first sense of danger. On a hill high above the meadow, their muzzles pointed at the stars, three gray wolves stood howling — not with the savage cries of the kill, nor the impatient voicing of hunger, but sad and mournful howls that gave way to high-pitched yappings of glee. Something about this savage serenade made El Blanco tremble and lie very still.

Later came the noises of small animals, of rats and mice and rabbits, scurrying through the thickets. A sudden scream of agonized fear made El Blanco raise his head. The sound came from a bush not twenty feet from where he lay. It was the death cry of a rabbit, caught by a fox — the first and last time the rabbit would ever use its voice. El Blanco's mother whirled and stared at the bush, but all was silent again.

High in a tree a big owl hooted; the hooting went on and on. Bats dipped and darted; they were hunting for mosquitoes and other flying insects. El Blanco relaxed. He was very tired after walking so far on his first day out in the big world. The mare stood guard while he slept. She would sleep after the sun came up the next day, while El Blanco was taking a daytime nap.

El Blanco was very hungry when he awoke the next morning. Seeing his mother grazing nearby, he scrambled to his feet and bounded to her, eager for her warm milk. Later the two moved on downcountry. The mare stayed out in the open, stopping often to crop the wild grass. During these halts El Blanco would race across the field. Once he flushed a large rabbit out of a bush. The rabbit leaped across the meadow with El Blanco hightailing after it, a frisky young colt enjoying

the race. When the rabbit vanished into a thicket
in the shade of some big trees, El Blanco started
to plunge in after it, but stopped when he heard
his mother's loud, sharp whinny. Instinctively, then,
the foal whirled and charged back to his mother.
He had much to learn about dangers around him.
If he survived, it would be because his mother had
kept a close guard over him.

As the days passed, El Blanco's legs became
sturdy and his speed increased. His chest widened;

he was developing the powerful lungs he would need for long, fast runs. Mare and foal moved down through valleys and grassy slopes toward the jungle. The forests were denser here, with very few open meadows. For a long time the mare and foal followed a stream. Its clear water was good to drink, and grass grew tall along its banks. El Blanco liked it for another reason too. He would charge down the shallow stream bed at top speed, his hoofs making the water fly in all directions.

One day he was racing along midstream, when suddenly he plunged into a deep pool, and the water closed over his head. Kicking and lashing, he swam to the bank, where his mother stood watching. The little colt whinnied shrilly. He had found out that he could swim!

Soon after this great discovery, he ate grass for the first time. He was only imitating his mother, but he liked the grass and ate more of it. It was an important step toward becoming independent.

Several weeks later El Blanco met some other wilderness dwellers. His mother was grazing in a meadow. A wind came up, blowing the tall grass into waves, like the waves of a sea. El Blanco dashed across this sea of grass, racing with the wind and waves. As he dodged around a bush, he found himself face to face with two fawns. Their mother had gone to drink at a stream nearby. She had left the fawns hidden in a thicket, but they had ventured out. And because El Blanco was between them and the underbrush, they ran out into the meadow. El Blanco dashed after them. The fawns had no fear of the colt. They danced about, and he bounded along with them. They were having a fine time when the doe came back. Her instinct was to protect her fawns, and so she charged the colt. Surprised, El Blanco whirled around and hurried back to his mother.

Wolf Kill

E L BLANCO WAS GROWING UP. He ate mostly
grass and tender shoots now, and he was
showing other signs of independence too. He spent
less time at his mother's side, and often wandered
off by himself. The mare still kept her eye on him,
but no longer insisted that he stay close to her.

One morning he trotted up a hill to have a look
at the scene on the far side. As he neared the top,

four buzzards swooped low over him and then disappeared from sight. They were ugly birds, with red, wrinkled heads, bare necks, and cruel beaks. Instinct told El Blanco that these birds were not his friends.

Galloping up the last few yards, he halted on the crest of the hill. Below him was something he had never seen before: the half-eaten carcass of a yearling colt. It lay in a circle of trampled grass, with a dozen buzzards tearing at it. El Blanco snorted and charged forward. As he approached, the buzzards ran awkwardly from the carcass, screaming their anger. They flapped their wings hard, to lift their gorged bodies into the air, and took off.

Now that El Blanco was close to the dead horse, he felt a sudden wave of fear. He backed away and whinnied loudly for his mother, who came galloping over the hill. She sniffed at the carcass and smelled the wolf scent, for it was a wolf kill. Disturbed, the mare lifted her head and looked around. On a far ridge she spotted three big gray wolves. They were loping toward a grove of trees, and she remained motionless until they vanished into the timber.

With the wolves gone, the mare sniffed at the carcass again. She was excited, for the dead colt meant that there were other horses in the vicinity. But fear of the wolves kept her from whinnying. She trotted on to higher ground. El Blanco stayed at her side, sensing the excitement and fear in the mare. When she halted and stood looking into a valley, he stood still and looked too.

The valley was deep, with a high ridge curving above it. Soon El Blanco saw the herd of wild horses — almost as soon as the mare did. The herd was running up a slope toward the high ridge, driven by a big sorrel stallion. The mare became so excited that she whinnied eagerly, forgetting about the wolves. Then she started off at a gallop, and El Blanco ran along at her side. Her only thought was to overtake the herd and join it.

As El Blanco and his mother galloped below the timber, the wolves burst from cover, alerted by the mare's call. This was the kind of situation that wolves preferred. They would often range close to a wild herd, waiting for a mare and her colt — or for a lone colt — to become separated from the herd. With the stallion too far away to protect them, the horses were easy victims.

The instant the wolves appeared, the mare shifted her course and cut back toward a rocky ledge. The wolves came leaping down the slope, their red tongues lolling over white fangs. Their leader, an old she-wolf, sounded the cry of the kill, and the two others took it up. El Blanco was the she-wolf's target, but she knew the mare would fight to the death for her colt. The two young wolves fanned out on either side of the she-wolf.

The mare had to get to the rocky ledge, where her flanks would be protected. Alone she could easily make it, but she had to keep her pace down to El Blanco's. He did not need any urging, and strained every muscle in his sturdy legs.

One of the wolves swerved and leaped toward El Blanco, intending to slash a tendon in his rear leg. El Blanco pressed close to the mare's shoulder as her hoofs flashed out, smashing against the wolf's chest. The wolf went rolling into the path of the she-wolf, who had to leap aside. This gave the mare and El Blanco time enough to reach the

ledge. There they whirled and faced their killers.

The she-wolf hesitated. The wolf that had been kicked was badly battered and limping. She herself could no longer attack on the flank, for the mare's powerful hoofs were deadly weapons in a head-on conflict. The third wolf would leap at them, then retreat, snarling. He had seen that the powerful mare could be dangerous, and he was cautious about getting too close.

El Blanco whinnied defiantly. Now that he and the mare held the wolves at bay, his courage returned. The instincts of a wild stallion were strong in him, but he did not yet quite dare to charge the wolves.

The she-wolf sat down and stared at El Blanco; the injured wolf lay down beside her. Only the third wolf continued the attack, often barely

leaping clear of the mare's lashing hoofs. Finally he too sat down, licked his lips hungrily, and whined. The she-wolf snarled at him. After an hour or so, the wolves got up and went slowly back toward the timber on the ridge. El Blanco and his mother watched intently until they had disappeared into the woods.

The herd of wild horses had now moved far beyond the high ridge. If the mare tried to follow them, the wolves would attack again. So when she moved away from the protection of the ledge, she headed downcountry toward the jungle, running swiftly with El Blanco at her side. The wolves did not attack again. It was summer, a time of plenty, and they were not desperately hungry.

The mare ran for several miles. She did not slow to a trot until the timbered hill that sheltered the wolves was out of sight. Finally the mare and colt reached a grassy meadow. Here they stopped and settled down to graze.

The Jaguar

THE PRESENCE OF WOLVES worried the mare. When she was with a herd, the stallion always watched for these enemies and attacked them. Now the safety of her colt depended upon her alone. She kept moving steadily downcountry, seeking a haven from the gray killers. The days became hotter, and the nights warmer and more humid. The weather bothered her, but she did not stop her journey downward.

As the days lengthened into weeks, El Blanco grew strong and fleet. He would often race off by himself, his small hoofs flying over the grass. He would circle a meadow, always returning to his mother when she called to him. He still needed her to protect him from enemies, and to teach him what she had learned during her lifetime. But when it came to food, he could live without her. The broad meadows furnished him with grass and tender shrubs; streams and springs gave him water to drink. He was happy and carefree, and forgot his terror of the wolves. In these lowlands he met no other predators. The small killers avoided him, and there were no big ones about.

The first signs of the jungle appeared one morning when El Blanco and his mother were moving down a gentle slope toward a swamp. Spanish moss hung from the trees above them, and clumps of palmetto lifted spiked spines to the sky. The underbrush grew dense, and thick vines made the going at times impenetrable.

Something about the low-lying swamp disturbed the mare, and she wanted to move on to the hill beyond it. El Blanco was some distance behind. He had stopped to watch an odd new animal waddle into the open. It was a strange creature, without hair or fur, covered by a round, bony shell formed in sections. El Blanco had never before seen an armadillo. Curious, he thrust his muzzle down to investigate. To El Blanco's surprise, the armadillo promptly made himself into a hard-shell ball.

El Blanco nudged the ball, and it rolled down a little slope and into a thicket. The colt snorted and dashed after it, thrusting his head into a spiny bush. The armadillo was no longer in sight. It had unrolled and made off deeper into the undergrowth. El Blanco stamped about, snorting loudly. He was pleased to have routed the animal, and he wanted to find it and chase it. He trotted along the wall of bushes, peering into the deep green gloom.

The mare, meanwhile, had reached the swamp, and stood hesitating at the edge. Its greenish water was filled with slime and smelled of rotting vegetation, but here and there hummocks dotted the surface, spaced several yards apart. The leap from one to the other would not be too great for El Blanco to manage. The mare leaped to the nearest hummock. It was actually a small floating island, and it shook and moved under her feet. She looked back and whinnied, then leaped to a second hummock.

At that moment a terrible roar shattered the silence — the roar of the jaguar, the most savage killer in the jungle. It was the first time the mare had heard a jaguar's cry of the kill, but instinctively she knew that a terrible danger was threatening her. She looked toward the far bank and saw the black-spotted cat leap from cover. His first spring carried him many yards, and he roared again as his pads landed on the soft earth. Swiftly he gathered himself for the final leap.

The mare whirled in fright. She lost her footing,

slid off the hummock, and floundered in the muddy water and slime. Instantly the jaguar was upon her. Unlike some big cats, he did not avoid the water; he was perfectly at home in a swamp.

Up in the meadow, El Blanco heard the roar and was terrified. He knew it came from the swamp, so he turned and raced toward the jungle and cover. He had gone only a few yards when he heard the second roar, and few moments later the agonized cry of his mother. In a panic, he fled still more swiftly. Then he stopped at the edge of the dense woods and whinnied desperately for the mare.

But when he looked back, he saw her lying helpless under the jaguar's attack, and the full instincts of a wild stallion rose up in the colt. He felt an urge to rush back and attack the killer, to save his mother. With a small, shrill scream he charged back down the slope to the swamp. The jaguar was dragging his mother, still battling weakly, from the swamp. Her cries now were faint.

El Blanco leaped toward the first hummock. His jump was short; he landed in the sucking slime and struggled to get back on solid ground, but

the oozing mud engulfed him. When his small
hoofs reached for solid ground, he missed by
inches. The more he struggled, the deeper he
sank into the muck which dragged at his legs and
body. He still wanted to fight the jaguar, but now
he was faced with a battle to save his own life.
Slowly, inch by inch, he moved toward the bank.
One hoof touched it, then the other. He needed
all his strength to pull his body from the grip of
the swamp. Gradually he freed himself, and at
last, plastered with mud and slime, he stood
trembling on the bank.

There was no sign of the mare or the jaguar. El Blanco whinnied wildly, shook himself, and called again. When there was no answer, he lay down and rolled on the ground to rid himself of the slime. The rough grass cleansed his coat, but it did not remove the stench of the swamp. Slowly he walked along the edge of the swamp. He was afraid to cross it, but he wanted to find his mother. Again and again he called, but there was no answer.

Tired and bewildered, the colt halted finally on the bank. He stood looking across the swamp toward the woods where the jaguar had vanished. He stood there, perfectly still, for a long time, until he saw a tawny form move across a small glade. The big cat, heavy with food, was making its way into deep cover, where it would sleep through the day.

El Blanco watched uneasily until the jaguar had disappeared. He was alone now in a world that contained more than one ruthless enemy. And he had had little training in the things he must do to survive. He was hungry, and so he started feeding, never thinking that he must put distance between himself and the killer. A wise horse would have left the jaguar's range immediately. But El Blanco did not know this. He simply went about satisfying his hunger.

When he had eaten his fill, he started back up the slope, seeking the spring where he and his mother had drunk earlier that morning. He trotted fast, looking back often and calling urgently. At the spring he drank, then lay down for a nap. He lay in the open, and his white color made him visible to any passing animal. But luck was with him; no killer came that way during the two hours that he slept.

On His Own

EL BLANCO WAS ALONE at the edge of the
jungle. He had had too little experience in
his brief life to know that the jungle was not the
place for a horse. He should have turned back to
the real horse country — the mountain meadows.
But the memory of the wolves, and the jaguar he
had seen at the swamp, kept him moving ahead,
and so he entered the green twilight of the jungle.

He found himself in a strange world, where every growing thing fought toward the sunlight, and the undergrowth teemed with creatures he had never seen before. High above his head were gaudy birds and swarms of brightly colored butterflies. As he made his way along a game trail that led through the thick undergrowth, he heard the screaming of parrots and macaws from the branches overhead.

Finding food and water in the jungle was not easy. There were few open grassy places. Rain fell regularly, and the air was humid and moist, but the springs were hidden under vines. Then he followed a side trail that led him to a pool. The water tasted of rotting leaves, but it was cool and refreshing, and he drank deeply.

Not far from the pool, he discovered a little clearing where the grass grew tall and green. He started to feed, and grazed until nearly sundown. Then, looking for a place to sleep, he saw a tree with large limbs extending low over the ground. It looked like an ideal shelter, and he settled himself under one of the huge boughs. He did not know that on the limb, its color blending with the color of the tree, was stretched a boa, the largest of all the jungle snakes. It was asleep, resting until it became hungry. For three days it had been here, digesting a small deer it had swallowed. In the morning it would awake and watch for game.

The night sounds of the jungle kept El Blanco awake and alert. Above the high-pitched hum of insects sounded the boom of a giant tree frog. A huge bat, the false vampire, wheeled through the branches of the tree, seeking out the hidden frog. El Blanco stirred restlessly at the distant scream of a jaguar attacking a tapir. He trembled with fear

as he heard the cry of a monkey snatched from its mother's side by an ocelot. It awakened the monkeys all around him. They shrieked angrily, and sleepy birds called out in protest. For a while the whole jungle was aroused by their clamor.

El Blanco rose to his knees, then sank back again, for he was exhausted. A pair of pampas cats, their striped sides showing faintly in the gloom, scurried past. They came so close to the colt they almost brushed against him. Then a savage wildcat halted close to the tree. Cautiously, because it had never seen a horse before, it stared at El Blanco. It stood motionless a few minutes, then moved on to seek smaller prey.

El Blanco finally went to sleep. He was awakened by a band of howler monkeys greeting the dawn. They were performing dizzying acrobatics, swaying from high perches, leaping from limb to limb. At the same time they bellowed, each trying to make more noise than the other. The howlers aroused the birds, who added their voices to the din. Day had begun in the jungle.

On the limb above El Blanco, the boa stirred. This was the big snake's hour for seeking prey. Its head lifted and swung downward as the long body rippled into movement. It eased itself further out from the limb, and then dropped softly to the ground, landing close to El Blanco.

The boa saw the horse and raised its head, ready to strike, but El Blanco, warned by instinct, got to his feet. The boa's head shot forward, seeking a hold that would crush the colt in its coils. El Blanco lashed out with his hoofs and struck the snake's head, hurling it back. With a defiant whinny, he leaped away from the tree and ran out into the clearing.

There he whirled around, but the boa was not following. It seldom attacked while on the ground. It needed to be high on a limb, from which it would drop down on its prey. El Blanco watched the brush sway as the boa slid into the tangled green mat of undergrowth. The colt whinnied again, then trotted out into the meadow, where he lowered his head and began to eat. After that he went to the pool and drank.

Several deer melted into the bush at his approach. On the other side of the pool a mother tapir, her striped and spotted baby at her side, stood watching. A long-snouted anteater, the tamandua, stared down at him from a tree, sinking its claws into the soft bark of a limb. It was harmless, but El Blanco did not know that. With its long thick tail and shaggy fur — yellowish white splashed with black — it *looks* quite dangerous. Cautiously, El Blanco edged away from the tree. Four white-lipped peccaries peered around a bush at him. These savage little jungle pigs were ready for a fight if the strange white creature bothered them.

El Blanco lowered his head to the pool. He drank deeply, snorted, and shook water from his muzzle. The peccaries squealed a challenge, but did not move. El Blanco turned away and trotted back along the trail.

Monkey Business

EL BLANCO stayed near the clearing for several weeks. He had wandered along many game trails, but he always came back here; it was the only place where he could find good grass. He could not eat the rank, dense growth under the trees. The beautiful orchids that grew in the shade, or the broad leaves of climbing vines, were not to his taste. He longed for open fields and meadows.

One morning he set out along a new trail. He traveled for several miles until he came to a place where the brush was not so dense. Huge trees shaded the ground, filling the woods with a soft twilight. El Blanco stopped to have a look around. Overhead were dozens of monkeys, chattering as they sat or swung from one tree to another.

In the highest branches was a band of howlers. These were long-tailed, reddish-coated monkeys with black faces and protruding brows. They would howl to warn of approaching enemies—like the ocelot or the harpy eagle — but their mouths were seldom closed. Some swung from the branches by an arm; others hung by the tail, swaying as they reached out for fruit to eat.

Lower down in the trees clustered the spider monkeys, with their long blackish arms, legs, and tails. They peered down curiously at the strange white creature that had come among them. One half-grown spider monkey climbed down to a low branch, and a gruff old fellow followed him.

El Blanco walked under the limb where the pair were sitting. The youngster leaned far forward for a good look at the colt, blocking off the old

monkey's view. Impatient, the old monkey gave the youngster a shove, knocking him off the tree. The youngster landed on El Blanco's back, gripped the colt's mane, and hung on. He was afraid of being on the ground, and thought he would wait until he had a chance to grab a limb and swing himself back into a tree.

Startled and frightened, El Blanco bolted, with the young monkey clinging to him. The colt charged down a steep slope toward a sharp turn. But as he rounded the turn at top speed, he found himself face to face with a big tapir. He was unable to stop, and instinctively hurdled over the tapir and went on.

The trail led straight to a narrow opening in the thick growth. El Blanco bolted through the opening; then suddenly planted his feet and slid to a halt. Before him was a river; he had almost plunged into it. The sudden stop sent the monkey sailing over El Blanco's head and into the river. The monkey thrashed toward shore, and was only a few feet away when the gaping jaws of an alligator rose from the water. With a frantic burst of speed, the monkey reached the bank just as the alligator's jaws snapped shut. The youngster

scrambled up, chattering excitedly, dashed to a tree, and climbed to a safe perch.

El Blanco stood still, too frightened to move. The alligator climbed out on the bank and lunged at him with open jaws. Suddenly El Blanco came to life. He leaped aside as the powerful jaws closed on empty air. The alligator pivoted, lashing its tail angrily. It had not given up, for it lay between the colt and the trail, cutting off his escape. The monkey screamed a warning, then turned and started swinging through the trees along the trail.

Remembering, perhaps, how he had hurdled the tapir, El Blanco charged the alligator, whose jaws had opened again. When the colt was almost on top of the alligator, he leaped high, jumping clear of the killer. He whinnied, then ran up the trail. He soon caught up with the monkey and followed him along a side trail. They stopped at a deep pool overhung with trees. El Blanco was thirsty, but he looked around with new wariness before he drank.

For a while the monkey sat in a tree, chattering and peering down at El Blanco. At last he lowered himself and approached the pool. He dipped one foot into the water, leaped back, and watched the water intently. He did this several times before he crouched and drank. After he had drunk his fill, he sat down. He folded his long thin arms and looked at El Blanco in a friendly manner.

El Blanco moved closer to him and extended his muzzle. The monkey hopped to his feet and raced around the colt. El Blanco ran after him, but the monkey darted up a tree and swung by his tail. He waved his long arms, chattering loudly, but he grew silent when he heard the other monkeys calling. For a moment he listened; then suddenly he was off, swinging from tree to tree.

El Blanco went trotting up the trail. That afternoon he found a small grassy meadow near the monkey grove, and only a short distance from the drinking pool. Here he stayed for a while, learning the ways of the jungle.

He met many new creatures, such as the three-toed sloth. This strange animal hung head down throughout the day and most of the night. It made its home in a tree so dense that it lived in damp gloom all its life. Moss grew on the sloth's back, blending it with the mossy tree. No animal bothered the sloth except its deadly enemies, the ocelot and the jaguar. Only these big cats could drag a sloth out of a tree once it had taken a grip with its long claws.

El Blanco learned to know many of the other jungle dwellers too — the red brocket deer, the tapirs that drank at the pool, a mother possum carrying her brood on her back, and a big frog-eating raccoon. Most of the creatures were not harmful, and El Blanco learned ways to avoid the dangerous ones, like the jaguar. The huge cat could be scented and heard before it was seen. It had a habit of making a coughing roar as it passed through the jungle. The sound served as a warning and alerted its prey.

The young spider monkey came closest to being El Blanco's friend. When the colt galloped through the grove, the other monkeys climbed high in the trees. But the youngster swung from a low limb and sometimes even dropped to the ground. He was full of curiosity, and one day he followed El Blanco down a narrow trail. The colt was running, and the monkey had all it could do to keep up with him. Suddenly El Blanco slid to a halt and jumped aside. The monkey stopped too, just in time to avoid the jaws of a boa. El Blanco lashed out at the snake with his hind feet, distracting it, and the monkey was able to escape to a tree.

And so the days passed, most of them peacefully enough. But there were times when danger threatened, and El Blanco learned to be on the alert for enemies. He also learned to pay attention to the warnings of the howler monkeys. They set up a terrible racket whenever an ocelot or a jaguar came near.

El Blanco was running through the forest one day and came to an open glade that promised grass. Howler monkeys were chattering in the trees, but as he entered the glade they began howling wildly. El Blanco looked around to see what had alarmed them. A few seconds later, a band of peccaries burst from the bush on all sides. He had invaded their rooting grounds.

A peccary is not large. But a hundred of them, attacking with sharp tusks and powerful jaws, can tear apart the largest animal in the jungle. They swarmed around El Blanco, squealing and frothing.

El Blanco leaped over the first pair, and struck out with his hoofs at others that were closing in. His leaps carried him over the pigs. But he needed some open space to land on, and get set for another leap. Twice, unintentionally, he landed on a squealing, slashing peccary.

If El Blanco had stood and fought, he would have been ripped to bits. Luckily he tried to get away. He leaped and dodged and ran until he was clear of the peccary herd. His shins were nicked and scratched, but he was not badly hurt.

As time passed, El Blanco became restless and felt an urge to move on. And one morning he headed for the uplands. This time he was moving toward the real horse country — the high grassy meadows above the jungle.

Toward the Hills

O N HIS WAY BACK to the tall-grass region, El Blanco turned down the game trail that led to the river. He had no particular reason for going there. But something seemed to draw him back to the place where he had lived for a while and had met the young spider monkey.

As he trotted down the trail, he came upon the remains of a tapir. The brush and shrubbery had been beaten down around where it lay, showing that the tapir had put up a hard fight. El Blanco sniffed. Mingled with the smell of death was the scent of a jaguar. The colt pawed the ground and snorted defiantly, then moved swiftly away. The jaguar might be lurking nearby, ready for another meal.

El Blanco raced along, ducking his head to avoid the overhanging vines and branches. He halted at the river. Hundreds of waterfowl floated on the slowly moving water, while hundreds more flew in the air just above it. Along the shore, wading birds stood or walked slowly about. Among them, in the shallow water, were flocks of scarlet ibis, with their brilliant plumage and long curving beaks. And near the shore the eyes of alligators watching for prey rose from the murky water.

El Blanco trotted along the shore a way. As he advanced, there was a great flapping of wings, and hundreds of birds took to the air. This pleased him, and he increased his pace to a gallop. He shook his head and whinnied loudly. His whinny was growing stronger; soon it would be the fighting scream of a full-grown stallion.

El Blanco stopped at a spot where the foliage hung low over the water. Hearing a sound behind him, he wheeled about and saw a red brocket doe come out of the bush. Very young and very thirsty, she walked swiftly toward the river. She seemed inexperienced, and the instinct of the herd stallion prompted El Blanco to warn her of danger. When she lowered her head, he whinnied shrilly and galloped toward her. The startled doe raised her head — and just in time. From the water the open jaws of an alligator were reaching for her muzzle. The doe whirled and fled back to the bush.

El Blanco stamped his feet, but the alligator refused his challenge and sank below the surface of the water. He galloped on to the monkey grove, where he slowed to a trot. The young spider monkey swung down from the trees and hopped after him. At the edge of the grove, the monkey sat down and watched the white colt vanish into the heavy growth.

El Blanco traveled all that day. Not until evening did he find a grassy clearing. He ate, then bedded down for the night in the open. When morning came he moved on, keeping to a steady pace. At last the dense foliage of the jungle began to thin out.

Finally El Blanco left the jungle altogether. He was re-entering the area near the swamp where his mother had been killed. He had no memory of this place, but he sensed a difference in the air from that of the steamy jungle. The smell in the wind blowing off the grassland filled him with a sudden eagerness. Dashing madly into a big meadow, he circled it several times before he settled down to feed. Then, at the base of a rocky ridge, he discovered a cold spring where he could drink. This was ideal country for a horse.

It was winter, but except for more rain and cooler nights, the climate was little different from that of summer. The grass stayed green, and during the day the sun was warm. Then spring came, and with it came a change in El Blanco. He was no longer a colt; he was a full-grown horse, with a powerful, magnificent body. He was restless, and often he stood on high ground and whinnied a challenge into the wind. His cry was the scream of a full-grown stallion.

One morning he galloped down to the spring

to drink as usual. He had come here so many times that he did not suspect danger. He knew no alligators lurked in the water, and he had never heard the cry of a jaguar here. But he was a creature of the wild, and never completely unwary. He lowered his head to drink, but quickly pulled it up again. His eye had caught a glimpse of movement on the ledge above.

He whirled and reared, just as a jaguar came at him. The big cat had been stretched out on the ledge, waiting for prey. Now it was leaping, its paws spread wide, its jaws gaping, showing its white fangs. It had not expected to be met by lashing hoofs, but now it could not check its attack.

El Blanco's hoofs smashed into the jaguar's face, hurling it backward, stunned. El Blanco felt no fear. He was a stallion facing a deadly enemy, and he was filled with rage and a desire to kill. He leaped forward, and brought his hoofs down upon the helpless jaguar before the big cat could roll aside. The hoofs came down, again and again. Soon the jaguar lay limp and lifeless in the bloody grass. El Blanco went on smashing at it until he was out of breath. At last he stopped, screamed triumphantly, then whinnied.

Bending down to the spring, he drank deeply. Without a glance at the dead jaguar, he trotted back to the meadow. The battle had made him feel his strength and power. He grazed only a short time, and then trotted away. Before him lay the ridges and mesas of the high country where he was born. Following a ridge, he raced upward and went on.

That evening he fed in a meadow bordered on one side by a timbered hill and on the other by a rocky wall. In the wall, about six feet above him, a cave opened from a shelf. He looked at the cave wonderingly, then moved out into the meadow toward the wooded slope.

By this time the trees were casting long shadows. Several silent gray forms crept out of the woods and followed the shadow of a pine tree to a brush-covered rise near El Blanco. He had his back to the rise and did not see the three wolves. They crouched in the brush, watching El Blanco closely. They were expert hunters, always ready to attack a lone horse. One of them left the rise and circled about, keeping low in the grass. It moved silently until it was below El Blanco. Then it crouched and waited.

The other two wolves suddenly broke cover and leaped toward the stallion, sounding the cry of the kill. El Blanco raised his head and snorted. He reared, so that he would be in position to meet the attack with his hoofs. At the same moment the third wolf leaped. It would try to sever a tendon in the horse's hind leg and make him helpless. El Blanco caught a glimpse of him, leaped far to one side, and ran toward the cliff. With the wolves snapping at his heels, he jumped to the ledge in one leap. The lead wolf also leaped, and got a foothold on a loose rock on top of the ledge. The rock rolled off and crashed into the wolf as it hit the ground. A second wolf leaped up, and El Blanco's hoofs sent him flying out into the meadow.

The two crippled wolves dragged themselves away. The third, a she-wolf, snarled and whined. She would not attack, but neither did she want to give up the prey. But after standing there awhile, she trotted away after the other two wolves.

El Blanco bedded down for the night in the cave. It was a safe shelter, but he would leave it and move on in the morning. He had met the deadliest killers in this part of the country, and had proved that he could master them. He did not fear them, and now nothing would keep him from seeking his own kind.

Herd Stallion

AFTER HIS ENCOUNTER with the wolves, El Blanco became more wary and watchful. He kept an eye on wooded slopes with heavy underbrush, and on any other place that gave cover to the gray killers. He moved on toward the high country, keeping to the ridges except when seeking water.

One clear, sunny morning, he stood on a rocky ridge overlooking a valley. Glancing down, he tossed his head and whinnied loudly; far below, grazing near a stream, was a herd of horses. A dozen mares were loosely bunched together, half of them with colts at their side. One horse stood alone on a rise. It was the herd stallion, a veteran of many seasons, tough and wise.

El Blanco leaped forward, sliding and slipping as he plunged down the steep slope. He raced down a deep ravine without slowing his pace, and ran up the far side. Coming out on a sloping mesa, he halted for a moment to sound a ringing challenge. The scarred veteran, a big sorrel, answered El Blanco's challenge at once. Fighting off young stallions was no new experience to him. None of them ever tried to return after he had battered them with his hoofs and ripped them with his teeth. The sight of a strange stallion always filled him with savage fury, and he charged across the meadow, screaming as he ran.

El Blanco knew little about this kind of fighting. He had only instinct to guide him, and a burning desire to take over the sorrel's herd. But his young strength made up for his lack of experience. Screaming, he laid back his ears, bared his teeth, and charged.

The two stallions came together with a jarring impact. The sorrel was the heavier; his weight set El Blanco back on his heels. Both reared and lashed out with smashing hoofs, slashing with their teeth as they closed. El Blanco knew no tricks. He just kept coming on, trying to smash his enemy.

The sorrel was wise in the ways of battle. He sidestepped to get at El Blanco's unprotected side and shoulder, avoiding the white stallion's lashing hoofs. El Blanco pivoted, but not before the sorrel's kicks had battered his shoulder and staggered him. He charged in, only to be met by flailing hoofs which fended off his blows.

Again the sorrel sidestepped and feinted. Again El Blanco felt smashing blows and teeth ripping at his neck. He almost went down, but somehow he managed to leap back. It was the first backward step he had taken, and it aroused a terrible fury in the sorrel. He plunged in, rearing and lashing out, determined to defeat the white stallion.

El Blanco recovered, lunged forward, and the two horses closed in on each other. Blood flowed freely. El Blanco's teeth had sunk into the sorrel's neck and face, and his own muzzle was ripped and

torn. The smell of blood filled both fighters with a new rage. El Blanco pressed the fight, giving the sorrel no chance to get set for a new attack. And El Blanco could no longer be fooled by the trick of sidestepping. When the sorrel leaped aside, he pivoted and lashed out first. His hoofs caught the unprotected ribs of the old stallion, staggering him. Instantly El Blanco was on him, lashing and ripping. And this time it was the sorrel that gave ground to the challenger.

The stiffening muscles of the aging sorrel were no match for El Blanco's young strength and energy. He struggled to defend himself, but El Blanco smashed aside his flailing hoofs. For the first time in his life the sorrel knew that he had to retreat or die. He tried desperately to break off the fight, but the raging El Blanco would not let him.

Suddenly the sorrel whirled and retreated, with El Blanco following close behind. The mares and colts bunched together and watched their leader flee. As the sorrel staggered over a hill, El Blanco halted and screamed his triumph. Then he saw two big gray wolves slip out of a thicket and leap after the sorrel. They had found a cripple who

could not fight back, and they would track him mercilessly.

The sight of the wolves aroused a new kind of fury in El Blanco. He was now the protector of the herd, and the wolves were enemies to be destroyed. Hearing his scream, they looked back and saw him charging at them. This was no cripple, but an angry herd stallion eager to stamp them into the ground. They broke from the sorrel and raced for cover on rocky slope. El Blanco let them go, not knowing that he had saved the life of the sorrel. He whirled and ran back over the hill to become the leader of the herd.

The mares watched with interest as their new leader came toward them. One filly, as though to test El Blanco, galloped away toward a stand of timber. Instinct told El Blanco what to do. He raced after the filly and soon overtook her. His teeth nipped at her rump, as he shouldered her around and sent her flying back to the herd. Bearing down then upon the other mares, El Blanco sounded a loud call, and the whole herd was off, running wildly. He crowded them, nipping sharply at those that hung back and racing ahead to guide the lead mares.

He kept the herd moving upward across mesa country. He allowed them to graze, but watched warily while they cropped the grass. He had a responsibility now — to protect the colts and the foolish fillies from lurking wolves. None could be allowed to stray very far from the herd.

The course which El Blanco followed seemed aimless, but it was taking him toward the rocky rim overlooking the valley where he was born.

Home Valley

IT WAS BRIGHT MORNING when the herd reached
the rim overlooking El Blanco's home valley.
There were only two entrances to the valley — the
canyon at the lower end, and a narrow defile which
led down from the rim. As El Blanco stood looking
down the defile, a rumble of thunder echoed off
the cliff wall. To the west a great thunderhead was
building up, gleaming white on top and slate-gray

below. El Blanco pushed his herd into the defile and started the descent. The going was slow, because the narrow canyon bed was very steep and littered with loose boulders.

The herd was halfway down when a deluge of rain struck the cliff walls above. This was no ordinary rainstorm, but a cloudburst; and as the torrents of water hit the rocky slope, they built up to a flood. The rushing water loosened rocks and sent them tumbling down the defile. These loosened other rocks, until an avalanche was in the making.

El Blanco heard the roar of the flood and screamed at the mares. He lashed at them and sent them stampeding down the canyon. The

avalanche pursued his flying hoofs, but he managed to swing the herd out of the defile onto the safety of a ledge. There the horses stood, watching the avalanche hit a curve in the canyon. The air was filled with the angry roar of the slide, punctuated by crashes of thunder.

The storm soon swept over the valley and was gone, and the sun shone again. But now there was only one exit from the valley. The slide had piled up, completely blocking the defile.

The old man's cabin stood close to the ledge. He had come out of his house as the first raindrops fell, and he stood in the open, allowing the rain to drench him. He took off his sombrero, and the rain soaked his white hair and poured down his face. He raised his arms to the rain, the life-giving rain that would quench the thirst of a parched land and revive the shriveled stalks of corn. As the rain slackened a little, he saw on the ledge above him a magnificent white stallion standing guard over a herd of mares. The old man stared and winked the water out of his faded eyes. No, it was no dream. The stallion was real. The wild horse shook his head, sent a defiant whinny after the retreating storm, and started moving his herd down into the valley.

The old man watched the herd pass. His mind was busy calculating how much time had gone by since he had found the white colt in the temple. Yes, this could be the same colt he had saved from Lopez, the horse hunter. The colt would be a mature stallion now. Just as in the legend, El Blanco had returned on the wings of a storm. The old man was sure that he would stay, and that there would be an end to the seasons of drought. Happily he started toward his house. He must sharpen his hoe. With the ground moist and alive again, weeds would spring up in his corn patch.

Down in the valley, El Blanco was looking over the land. He did not know that this was a safe haven, free from enemies. But he sensed that this was the place he had been seeking. Now he must explore it. He must find spots where the herd could hide, and escape routes from the valley if they should need to leave it. He found the canyon at the lower end and explored it while the mares fed in the open. He came to the remains of the trap Lopez had once used. The scattered poles and the still upright posts meant nothing to him. But he did discover that this canyon would lead to open country below, and would therefore make a fine escape route.

Returning to the mares, he drove them up into the timber on the slopes which rose to the base of the cliffs. He made a complete circle around the valley, keeping close under the high rims. He located a big cave which could be used as a hiding place. Above the old man's house he halted to stare at the crumbling ruin of the ancient temple. He moved to the entrance and smelled the water of the spring inside, but he had no way of knowing that he had been born here.

The herd returned to the valley, and El Blanco discovered a hidden pool where the horses could drink. It was formed by a depression in the solid rock floor among the big boulders. The boulders fenced in the pool on three sides. On the fourth side was a narrow opening. El Blanco approached cautiously, remembering that water holes attract killers. But this was not the jungle; nor was it wolf country. No killers molested the herd as they moved in and drank.

Finding no trace of danger anywhere, El Blanco became a little less watchful. The herd roamed the grass meadows in the early morning, in the evening, and at night. When the sun was hot during the day, they sought the cool shade of the trees on the slope. This was truly a haven for horses.

Up on the slope the old man sat and watched the herd every evening. Mostly he watched the white stallion, and he often muttered a word of thanks for his return. The old man saw no reason why he could not be a Christian and still believe in the old stories. He was sure El Blanco was the legendary white stallion, master of storm and rain.

The old man made no attempt to approach the herd, although he could have ridden his burro into the valley. He did not have to be close to the white stallion to draw strength and contentment from him. Seeing him from afar was enough.

And so a week passed, and another week began. The corn in the old man's patch was growing tall. He no longer had to fear hunger. There would be corn and beans in his storeroom when fall came. He had stayed here in the face of starvation, and now he could remain here for the few years left to him.

Lopez Returns

THE OLD MAN SAT DROWSING in the sun on his doorstone, his sombrero pulled down over his face. The early-morning sunshine warmed his old bones, easing the aches that had built up during the night. He was awakened by a voice greeting him.

"Hi, old man!"

Opening his eyes, he shoved back the sombrero.

Before him, mounted on a horse, was Lopez, the wild-horse hunter. The old man's face froze, and fear stirred within him. Had Lopez come to hunt again?

Lopez swung out of the saddle. "I have much thirst."

The old man nodded toward a water jar with a gourd dangling from its neck. He watched Lopez as the stocky man helped himself to a drink. Judging from his battered hat, scuffed boots, and worn clothing, Lopez was not doing too well. And he was alone. If he had money, he would surely have hired helpers, as he had done when he first raided the valley.

Lopez saw how the old man was looking at him. "Times have been bad, old man. I have tossed my money away foolishly." He shook his head. "Now I want one more good band of horses. If I get them, I will pick up a nice piece of land and settle down."

"So," the old man answered. He had no intention of offering Lopez any help.

"Have you seen any horses in this valley?" Lopez's black eyes studied the old man carefully.

Slowly the old man shook his head. "These old eyes do not see so well." The old man did not want to lie, but he was desperate. At the same time he could not keep from glancing toward the timbered slope where he had seen El Blanco and the mares just before he dozed off.

Lopez noticed the look and turned. The old man stiffened and choked back a warning cry, for at the edge of the timber several mares and colts had appeared. A moment later more mares came out of the woods.

Lopez turned back to the old man. "Your eyesight is indeed bad," he said mockingly.

The old man got to his feet. He placed a hand on Lopez's arm as the hunter went toward his horse.

"No," he said pleadingly. "Leave them here. Find another valley."

Lopez impatiently shook off the old man's hand. "The horses are wild. They belong to anyone who can catch them."

"I have a few pesos saved. This money is yours if you will go." The old man's hands shook as his fingers searched inside his shirt for the leather pouch he carried there.

Lopez laughed and mounted his horse. "Keep your handful of pesos, old man. Good horses are worth real money."

The old man watched Lopez ride down into the valley at a gallop. Then he looked across toward the slope where the mares were grazing. He was glad that El Blanco had not shown himself. For a brief moment his heart lifted. Perhaps the white stallion had sensed danger and had gone away again. But no, that he could not hope for. Lopez would see him and capture him.

On his way to the canyon to examine his old trap, Lopez caught sight of El Blanco. The white stallion had come out of the woods and stood on a rise above his mares. His head was up, and his mane and tail flowed in the wind.

Lopez stopped and stared, hardly able to believe what he saw. Here was a horse that by itself would bring him, Lopez, enough money to set himself up on a ranch. He could keep the mares for breeding stock and buy or rent another stallion.

Slapping his leg, he said aloud. "At last my luck has changed."

Then he frowned. He had no helpers and no money to hire any. It would take much work to rebuild the trap. But he could do it. The canyon was just the right place to capture the horses. They would run for that exit if he headed them in that direction, and made the stallion stampede them. He roused his horse and rode toward the mouth of the canyon.

From his position on the slope, El Blanco saw

the mounted man and watched warily. He could not remember ever having seen a man, let alone a man on horseback. To him, the man was simply part of the horse. He moved to higher ground where he could look into the canyon. Lopez was dismounting and walking toward the scattered poles on the ground. So this strange, upright animal was not really part of the horse! El Blanco snorted. Whirling about, he sent a sharp warning down to the mares. He galloped to them and drove them into the woods.

El Blanco was not greatly troubled by the strange two-legged creature, but he meant to watch him. At the first sign of danger, the stallion would take his herd into hiding. But if the man left him alone and made no attempt to attack the mares, there would be nothing to fear.

For a week El Blanco watched where Lopez was working on the trap. The man did not bother the wild horses at all. In fact, he did not even seem to notice them. He camped at a distance from the big spring. He did water his horse there, though, so El Blanco led his herd to the spring only at night.

As for the old man, he spent most of his time sitting around and brooding. The weeds grew high in his corn patch, but he did not chop them down. He watched the progress Lopez was making in building the trap, and tried to think of a way to save the stallion and his herd. His old burro was too slow to stampede the herd out through the canyon before Lopez finished the trap. The ancient animal had not moved faster than a trot in years.

The old man had to admit that Lopez was a hard worker. He chopped down trees and cut poles. Because he had no spikes, he lashed the poles into place with vines and bark. The old man did not have to go down and look at the trap to know it would be strong. He could tell as much from the heavy poles and logs which Lopez had dragged down into the canyon.

From his perch on his doorstone the old man watched and waited. There was nothing else he could do. He could not go away and hide until the horses were captured and everything was over.

A Duel Begins

EIGHT DAYS after Lopez had come to the valley, El Blanco was still on guard. He watched Lopez ride up the slope past the spot where he usually stopped to cut his poles. El Blanco sounded a warning and quickly pushed the mares and colts into a heavy grove of trees. Then he stood watch again. Even after Lopez was out of sight he did not let the mares leave cover.

El Blanco's alertness was rewarded when he saw Lopez burst from cover above the herd's hiding place. Lopez was swinging a saddle rope as he galloped his horse down the slope. Believing that El Blanco would stampede the herd into the canyon, he stood up in his stirrups and shouted loudly. But what happened was something entirely different. El Blanco whirled and plunged into the grove. With an angry scream, the stallion sent the mares and colts up around the slope above Lopez. He would take the herd to one of the other hiding places he had found while exploring the valley. He himself galloped in the open to keep the mares from running for the floor of the valley. He wanted to stay in the timber up under the rims.

Lopez swung his rope and sent his horse racing toward El Blanco. His idea was to make the stallion turn and run in the other direction. But the jungle-trained El Blanco went charging ahead, just as he would have attacked a jaguar or a pack of wolves. Lopez's horse had mixed with wild stallions before, and it wanted no fight with this one. It dashed downhill, bucking and pitching. It was all Lopez could do to stay in the saddle. He was a fine horseman and had ridden many bucking broncos, but now his mount was wild with fear.

Meanwhile El Blanco swerved and raced after his herd. He pushed the mares up to a curve in the wall of the cliff. Here he kept them hidden in the dense timber that grew close to the rocky wall. While they fed on grass, he took a stand at a point from which he could watch the slopes below.

Lopez finally got his horse under control. Looking around, he saw that the ground had been softened by the rain, and that the herd had left a clear trail of hoof prints. He was a man who did not give up easily. His jaw set stubbornly, he took up the trail. El Blanco waited until Lopez started up the slope. Then he sent the herd around the rim and down to a small mesa that broke off into a deep arroyo — a dry stream bed. Lopez noticed the movement of the herd and changed his course. He meant to stay on the trail until the stallion decided to leave the valley.

For three hours El Blanco remained on guard while the mares fed. Running in the hot sun had made them thirsty, and they began to get restless.

El Blanco was busy cutting off a filly that tried to break away, when Lopez appeared. He burst out of a nearby grove, yelling wildly as he rode straight toward the herd.

El Blanco crowded the mares to the steep edge of the arroyo. Using his hoofs and teeth, he sent them plunging over the rim in a shower of stones and earth. They slipped and slid, but down the arroyo they went, with El Blanco close behind them. Like all wild horses, they were so sure-footed that even the colts reached the bottom safely.

Lopez pulled up at the edge of the arroyo, furious. For a few moments it had looked as though the herd was trapped and would head down an easy slope for the floor of the valley. He set his spurs and sent his protesting horse over the edge. His mount was no sure-footed wild horse, however, and it was carrying a heavy rider. Halfway down the slope it stumbled and fell. Lopez could do nothing but leap clear and roll to the bottom with his horse. As he stood up, the horse galloped away. Before going down the arroyo, Lopez had tied his reins securely around the saddle horn. This was an invitation for the horse to head for camp. Lopez knew that he would find the animal waiting for him there, but that did him no good now. He would have to walk.

Lopez angrily trudged along, sweat pouring from his face. He realized that he would have to change his plan. El Blanco was extremely cunning, and clearly did not intend to leave the valley.

Lopez knew all the tricks of hunting wild horses. He could, of course, shoot the white stallion; then the leaderless herd would be at his mercy. But he could not bring himself to do it. He was determined to capture the stallion, for it was the most magnificent horse he had seen in a lifetime of hunting wild horses. He decided to use a trick that had worked before. He would camp at the water hole and keep the horses from drinking. Thirst would force them to try to leave the valley.

From his doorstone, the old man had been watching the chase. He was pleased when he saw Lopez's riderless horse come galloping back. Later Lopez himself walked into the camp. The old man wondered whether the hunter would give up in disgust now. Well, he would have to wait and see. The old man stayed on his doorstone, watching for signs that Lopez was breaking camp.

By evening the old man knew that Lopez was not giving up. He was moving his camp to the big spring, and the old man knew at once what the hunter had in mind. Greatly disturbed, the old man stood up and stared down into the valley. There would be a moon that night, and perhaps he would be able to help the white stallion. He took down the hatchet hanging on the wall of his house. Testing the blade with his thumb, he shook his head. He looked around until he found a flat piece of sandstone. Sitting down again, he sharpened the blade of the hatchet.

Night Chase

THE OLD MAN rode into the canyon on his burro. In the moonlight he could see Lopez's trap. Its gate was held open by a prop. Attached to the prop was a rope, the other end of which disappeared behind a bush on a shelf. Sliding off the burro, the old man walked slowly to the gate. With the sharp blade of his hatchet, he chopped through the wrappings which held the gate poles in place. He finished the job as quickly as he could, then mounted his burro and rode back to his house.

High on a slope, El Blanco was having trouble keeping the mares together. They were in desperate need of water, and he finally started them down toward the big spring. They moved fast. Their hoofs loosened rocks that bounded down the steep slope, awakening echoes in the still night.

As the herd neared the spring, El Blanco saw Lopez's campfire. Lopez was seated beside it, with his tethered horse standing nearby. El Blanco circled the herd and sent it back up the slope. As he galloped away, Lopez got to his feet, looked into the night, and listened.

El Blanco halted the herd on a ledge. He whinnied defiantly, but he was troubled. He could not get the mares to water, and without water they could not stay in the valley. He would have to use his escape route. He began to move them down again, toward the canyon. After so much running, all the horses were tired, especially the colts. They moved slowly, blowing and snorting, unwilling to turn away from the spring. Lopez heard the hoofbeats and knew where the herd was going. His horse was already saddled. He bridled it, mounted, and rode off to the canyon. He would hide behind a bush, ready to close the gate after the herd had entered the trap.

The herd approached the mouth of the canyon at a walk. El Blanco was suspicious and stopped the mares. Tired and thirsty as they were, they did not dare to risk his anger. They stood watching as he galloped into the canyon — and into the trap. He slid to a halt when he reached the barrier below the gate, staring at it. At the same time, crouching behind the bush on the ledge, Lopez smiled. The stallion was in the trap at last. And once he had captured the stallion it would be easy to round up the mares. They would scatter, but they would not go far from the big spring. Lopez pulled the rope. The prop fell, and the gate swung shut.

Whirling around, El Blanco charged straight at the gate. He leaped high, and as he hit the top, the gate seemed to explode. Poles flew in every direction. Free of the trap, he raced up the canyon while Lopez stared.

Quickly Lopez climbed down from the ledge and examined the broken gate. He knew at once what had happened. The lashings on the gate poles had been cut — and there was only one person who could have done it. Anger boiled up within him. Muttering to himself, he ran to his horse, which he had hidden in a thicket. He mounted and galloped away.

El Blanco drove the mares to high, timbered ground. No matter how desperate they were for water, he must keep them away from the man in the valley. All night he held the herd at that spot, and in the morning he looked down toward the spring. There was no sign of Lopez nor of his camp. Cautiously, watching for the man, El Blanco finally allowed the herd to move into the valley.

Lopez had spent the night repairing the gate

of the trap. When he had finished his work, he rode up to the old man's house and warned him not to interfere again. His revolver was strapped to his waist, and he made it clear that he would not hesitate to shoot anyone who tampered with his trap in the future. After that, he rode back down into the valley and hid near the spring. He had changed his plan again. He would let the thirsty horses drink their fill. Once they were bloated with water, he would be able to handle them easily.

As the herd approached the spring, El Blanco held back. He was as thirsty as the mares, but he was their leader and had to be on the watch for danger. The mares pressed forward and sucked in the cold water greedily. They gorged themselves until they were heavy and clumsy with the overload.

Lopez waited, hoping that the white stallion too would drink. But when the mares began to move away from the spring, he could wait no longer. Breaking from cover, he rode toward the herd. El Blanco screamed and charged at the mares. He could not make them stampede, no matter how he slashed and pushed and battered at them. They were heavy with water and could not go faster than a trot. El Blanco stayed with the herd until Lopez was upon him, then broke and galloped away.

A smile of triumph on his face, Lopez waved his hat at the old man, who was sitting on his doorstone. Then he herded the mares into the trap and fastened the gate. He still had to catch the white stallion, but he was confident. By the time he got back to the spring, El Blanco would surely have gorged himself with water. As Lopez rode back into the valley, he was already making plans for a ranch of his own. He knew horses, and he would build up the best horse ranch in this part of Mexico.

El Blanco had made his way to high ground, where he stood watching the valley. He had not abandoned the mares; instinct told him that the time to regain his herd was at night. Now he could not return to the big spring, and must look elsewhere for water. His eyes on the rider below, he shook his head and stamped his feet. Suddenly he remembered where he could find water without going to the big spring. Turning, he moved swiftly up the slope.

He approached the temple cautiously, sniffing

the air. There was no scent of man. Across a low barrier at an opening in the broken walls, he smelled the water. El Blanco leaped the barrier and trotted over to the small spring; it trickled into a basin hollowed out of a large rock.

The basin held only a small amount of water, and it was this that saved the white stallion from drinking too much. After sucking up all the water in the basin, he had to wait for the thin trickle of the spring to fill again. When it was half full, he drank again. He did this several times, waiting patiently, with his head down, for the basin to fill. He needed rest badly. After drinking enough to quench his thirst, he lay down.

Lopez was again hiding near the spring, waiting for the stallion. Several hours passed, and he became worried. Perhaps the stallion had found another way out of the valley and had run off. Mounting his horse, Lopez started for the spot where he had seen the stallion when he rode up from the canyon. He would pick up the big fellow's trail and find out what had happened to him.

Showdown

El Blanco's tracks led Lopez to the ruins of the temple. He did not really expect to find the stallion trapped inside. That would be too much to hope for. Still, he could not afford to overlook anything. Dismounting quickly, he took his saddle rope and walked to the opening in the wall.

Peering over the barrier, he almost shouted with joy. There was El Blanco, hemmed in by the walls of the temple. The stallion had already scented the hunter. Now he saw him, and shaking his head, he whinnied savagely. Lopez grinned. He had roped and choked down many an outlaw horse in a corral no bigger than the temple. True, there were a few obstacles — the slabs of stone leaning against the walls or scattered over the floor, where they had fallen when the roof caved in.

Lopez stood on the barrier. He planted his feet wide and swung his rope, shaking out a loop. He jumped down from the barrier and moved slowly toward El Blanco. The stallion snorted and pawed the ground, but remained in the same spot. This was exactly what Lopez had expected. Glancing around him, he saw a big slab of stone nearby. After he had dropped the loop around the stallion's neck, he would snub the rope on the big stone. El Blanco would fight the rope and be choked into submission. Lopez swung the loop, and it flew through the air, straight and true. As it dropped over the stallion's neck, he pulled in the slack.

But El Blanco was no ordinary outlaw. He had grown up in the jungle, and the instant he felt the rope he reared. Screaming savagely, he plunged forward, lashing out with his hoofs. Lopez jumped aside, the hoofs barely missing him.

El Blanco had become a raging killer. He wheeled and struck at Lopez, who dodged and leaped over a pile of rubble. The big hoofs smashed down close to his heels. Lopez found himself trapped in a corner, and dropped the rope. All he wanted now was to get out of the temple. He made a desperate leap to get past the horse, but the flashing hoofs sent him rolling across the rocky floor. Stunned, he pulled himself to his hands and knees. Less than a foot away was a stone slab leaning against the wall, with just enough space under it for him to crawl into. He scrambled under the slab, but his feet stuck out. He managed to get them under cover as the stallion's hoofs came down.

El Blanco attacked the stone slab, smashing down on it again and again. It cracked and settled a little; then part of it slid off, uncovering Lopez

from the waist up. El Blanco reared and struck, but the blow fell short. The rope, its loop still around his neck, had become wedged between two big stones. Stretched tight, it held El Blanco back, keeping him from getting at Lopez. He strained hard, but the rope cut off his wind, and he had to ease off. He threw his weight against it again, and it rubbed against the sharp rock. One strand was cut through, and then another.

As El Blanco strained against the weakening rope, the figure of a man appeared on the barrier. It was the old man, and he took in the situation at a glance. He immediately jumped down inside the temple, and Lopez shouted at him:

"Go back, old man! He will kill you!"

The old man did not answer Lopez. Instead, he spoke softly to El Blanco.

"Easy, mighty one," he said. "It is not good to take a life, even the life of a horse hunter."

As he talked, he quietly approached El Blanco. His hand touched the rope and moved along it toward El Blanco's neck. Lopez watched grimly. He had already given himself up for dead, and nothing could be done about it. But the old man was a fool, and would only get himself killed too.

The old man went on talking. "The gods are merciful, as you must know, being one of them. This man Lopez will make up for his sins."

His fingers had reached the loop around El Blanco's neck. The stallion flinched at his touch, but the old man's hands were gentle.

Lopez heard what the old man said. He realized that the old man believed the white stallion was a god. It gave him a strange feeling at first, and then a little hope began to stir within him.

The old man's fingers slowly loosened the loop. El Blanco took a deep breath, and the old man patted his neck reassuringly.

"It is better to be free," he said, "than to be held by a rope."

And swiftly he flipped the loop over El Blanco's head. El Blanco seemed to understand that he was free. He reared, and for a moment his hoofs hung over Lopez. Then he pivoted, and with a wild whinny he leaped to the barrier and over it, vanishing from sight. As the old man bent over Lopez, they heard El Blanco's wild cry and knew he was galloping into the valley.

With the old man tugging and pulling, Lopez slid from under the slab. He sat with his back propped against the wall, rubbing his skinned knees. The old man brought him some water from the spring in his battered old sombrero, and Lopez drank gratefully.

"I thank you, old man," he said, and it was plain that he meant it.

The old man stared at him. "You will leave the valley now? You will free his mares and go?"

Lopez smiled and shook his head slowly. "As I told you, I plan to settle down. This valley is a good place for raising horses." He paused and shook his head again. "You talked to him, and I listened. Why am I alive? Because he understood you. He shall have his freedom, but he must share his colts and fillies with me."

The old man looked at Lopez for a long time before he said, "I think he would do that."

"We'll get him used to us. He'll share. He won't want the young stallions, and he won't miss a few fillies."

"It could be that way," the old man said. "But why do you say 'we'?"

"I need a partner who has a way with horses, who can speak reason to them." Lopez laughed and thrust out his hand. "Help me to my feet, old man. We have much to plan."

The old man reached down and took Lopez's hand. Lopez stood up, and they started toward the barrier. When they reached it, Lopez stopped.

"For one thing," he said, looking around the temple of the storm god, "we'll need rain to keep the grass tall."

"We will indeed," the old man said.